WHICH WITCH IS WHICH

WHICH WITCH IS WHICH

by BARBARA CORCORAN

Atheneum / Escapade
New York

Library of Congress Cataloging in Publication Data

Corcoran, Barbara.
    Which witch is which.

    (Escapade)
    Summary: After a series of neighborhood
catnapping, including their own cat, inquisitive
twins follow a frightening old woman to an
abandoned house where they find both the cats
and danger.
    [1. Mystery and detective stories] I. Title.
PZ7.C814Wh 1983 [Fic]   83-3900
ISBN 0-689-31373-X

Cover art copyright © 1983 by Brad Hamann

Published simultaneously in Canada by
McClelland & Stewart, Ltd.
Composition by Westchester Composition Co., Inc.,
Yorktown Heights, New York
Manufactured by Kingsport Press, Kingsport, Tennessee
First Edition

For Jai Cloud-Song, princess of Siam

WHICH WITCH
IS WHICH

1

On the way home from school Jennifer and her twin brother Jack walked a block out of the way so Jack could look at the old house again.

"How do you know a witch lives there?" Jennifer said.

"I didn't say that. I said one of the kids that started the witch hunts lived there. Three hundred years ago."

"How do you know?"

"Mrs. Bennett said so. If you listened in class, you'd know." Jack was writing a paper on witchcraft for English.

Jennifer glanced around uneasily. She and her family had just moved to Salem from Dover, New Hampshire, and she wasn't used to all this talk about witches. People around here referred to them as if they were everyday people.

Jack stopped as they came near the house. "It looks haunted."

Jennifer studied the big, hip-roofed house with the peeling paint. "There was a nice lady in the garden the other day. She said hello."

"Probably a cover." Jack glanced at his sister. He didn't really believe in witches, but he liked to scare her.

Jennifer shivered. She wished she were safely home with her cat, Chloe.

"They got hung," Jack said, "the witches. Or squeezed between two slabs of granite." He went closer and leaned on the picket fence.

"I want to go home," Jennifer said.

"Oh, don't be a scaredy cat. It's just a house." She made herself stand still.

Whoever lived here took good care of the garden. There were still some asters and some late-blooming roses undamaged by the light frosts; and in the space for vegetables, there was a heap of golden pumpkins and squashes. But the house itself looked shabby and neglected. One of the windows in the front was cracked.

"They ought to get that window fixed," Jack said. "It's a gloomy-looking old house, isn't it."

"Yeah," Jennifer said. "Probably it's haunted."

They both jumped as a figure suddenly loomed up on their right, inside the fence. A tall, bony woman, dressed in a long faded black skirt and a man's shirt that hung on her as if she were a scarecrow, glared at them from small, unfriendly eyes.

"Git!" she said. She had a broken bamboo rake in her hands, and she waved it at them as if they were debris to be gotten rid of. "Git away from there."

Jennifer grabbed Jack's hand and ran.

When they were safely around the corner, she said, "That looks like the same woman that said hello the other day. How come she's so mad at us this time? We weren't doing anything." Now that she was safe, her fear turned to indignation.

Jack shrugged. "Some folks don't like kids hanging around."

Jennifer didn't say anything, but she had her

own answer to her question. If the woman was descended from that witch bunch, no doubt she was pretty witchy herself. She thought about broomsticks and black cats. But as they turned into their own street, she forgot all about witches and unfriendly old ladies. Her beloved Chloe was coming toward her.

"Chloe!" She held out her arms, and the cat jumped into them and lay on her back in Jennifer's arms, her legs sticking straight up, her orange and black throat throbbing with a welcome-home purr.

Their mother had cocoa and sugar cookies ready for them in the big, friendly kitchen.

"Has Chloe eaten?" Jennifer asked, knowing she had, because her mother never forgot.

"Yes, dear. I kept her in most of the day." She pointed to the *Salem News* that lay on the kitchen table. "There's a cat scare."

"Cat scare?" Jennifer grabbed the paper and read the headline her mother pointed to. "CAT THIEF STRIKES AGAIN." She gasped and clutched Chloe closer. "'The person who upset cat lovers last year is at his or her catnapping again. Mrs. Thomas Fullerton reports that her pedigreed

Burmese cat was snatched out of her yard sometime yesterday. The cat, whose name is Joyous Melody Harrison-Eagcr, was wearing a green, gem-studded collar and an i.d. disc with Mrs. Fullerton's phone number. A reward is offered.'"

Jack put a whole cookie into his mouth at once and said, with some difficulty, "A cat named *what?*"

"Joyous Melody Harrison-Eager."

"Pedigreed animals have complicated names," his mother said. "Don't swallow without chewing, Jack."

Jack washed down the cookie with a long drink of cocoa. "Here, Joyous Melody Harrison-Eager," he said, imitating someone calling a cat. "Here, kitty kitty Joyous Melody Harrison-Eager, honey."

"It's not funny," Jennifer said. "I think it's terrible. What kind of monster would steal somebody's cat?"

"A monster who wants to sell it and make a bundle," Jack said. "Be glad Chloe is an alley cat."

"She's not," Jennifer said.

"Sure she is. The animal shelter said so. They found her right after she was born. In an alley."

"Well, she can't help that."

Jack sighed. "Jen, you're so illogical."

Later in her room, with Chloe purring on her lap, Jennifer carefully smoothed down the velvety white patch on top of the cat's head. "Don't feel bad," she said. "You're not a real alley cat. I'm going to call you Chloe Happy Singer James. You've got as much right to a long fancy name as anybody."

Chloe bent one ear forward and then flicked it back again, to let Jennifer know she had heard.

2

The twins stood waiting in the front yard of the church while their mother talked to her new friend, Mrs. Eaton.

Her mother beckoned to her. "This will interest you, Jennifer. Jennifer loves cats, Mavis. Tell her what happened."

"I'm so upset," Mrs. Eaton said. "My cat has been stolen."

Jennifer gasped. "That's terrible!" She waved Jack over to her. "Mrs. Eaton's cat has been stolen."

"Gosh, that's awful," Jack said. "Any clues?"

"Not a one," Mrs. Eaton said. "She was in our fenced yard, and she never roams. She's been spayed, and she's a real homebody. Persians are, you know."

"A Persian," Jennifer said. "What color?"

"Sort of silver-blue. I'm offering a reward."

Another woman joined them and began talking to the twins' mother about the guild bake sale.

"Listen, Mrs. Eaton," Jennifer said, "we'll try to find your cat for you." She glanced at Jack, who nodded. "Give us your address and a short description, the cat's name, her tag numbers, whatever."

Mrs. Eaton pulled a tiny pad of paper and a silver pen from her purse and began to write. "Her name is Jasmine. She's three years old. She's such a lovely cat." Her eyes filled with tears.

"Don't you worry." Jennifer folded the piece of paper that Mrs. Eaton gave her. "We'll find Jasmine for you, somehow."

"I'll pay a reward," Mrs. Eaton said again. "I put it in the paper. Fifty dollars."

Jennifer blinked. Half of fifty dollars would buy Chloe the cat's bed she had seen advertised in a catalog. "We'll find Jasmine, don't worry."

On the way home, she said to her mother, "Poor Mrs. Eaton. She's really nice."

Her mother smiled. "I thought you'd like her. Cat people like each other, I've noticed."

"What we've got to do," Jennifer said later, when she and Jack were helping their father rake up the leaves in their yard, "is to figure out the thief's system."

Jack nodded. "His M.O."

"What?"

"His *modus operandi*. That's what they call it. It's Latin for 'how he works.' Most criminals use the same methods over and over. It usually traps them in the end, which goes to show you that criminals are not as smart as they think they are."

"How do you know?"

"How do I know what?"

"Never mind." Sometimes it discouraged Jennifer that her brother knew all kinds of things she hadn't heard of.

"Hurry up and finish," called their father, "and I'll take you out in the boat."

Jennifer showed him how efficient she could be, and within an hour they were chugging around Salem harbor in their old outboard. Offshore near

Salem Willows the motor died, and their father worked on it for twenty minutes before he got it going again. Maybe if they found Mrs. Eaton's cat, Jennifer thought, they should give Dad the money to get a new motor. This one, which had come with the house, was so old, it was always giving out, and one time they had had to get out the oars and row ashore.

"I'm glad we live close to the water now," Jack said. "When can we take the boat out alone, Dad?"

Their father looked hot and impatient. "Never. This old warhorse is too chancey."

"Never?" Jack looked upset. "Oh, come on, Dad. All the kids I know take their dad's boat out alone. Jarvis Haines even goes lobstering alone."

"Well, you aren't Jarvis Haines."

Jennifer took a deep breath of salt air and leaned back. Her brother might be smart about some things, but he wasn't smart about Dad. She had learned long ago not to ask for things when her father was tired or upset. Tomorrow when he was feeling better, he'd probably say they could take the boat out. She stepped on Jack's foot to warn him, but he only glared at her and said, "Ouch!"

When they came back to the wharf, she said, "We'll tie it up for you, Dad."

"All right. Be sure you do a good job with the lines."

She grinned as her father took the motor off the boat and stowed it away in the tiny boat house. Poor Dad. He wanted a sail boat so bad. And he talked about the old creaky outboard as if it were a fast, trim little cat boat.

Jennifer straightened up from tying the rope and read off the names of the boats that anchored here. She was trying to memorize them, just for fun. A big dory, with its paint peeling, looked as old as their own *Millicent F.*. She tried to make out the faded name on the dory. *Mercy W.*, that was it. The C was almost gone, but it was *Mercy* all right. She wondered whose boat it was.

"What we've got to do," she said on the way back to the house, "is to make ourselves a detective agency."

"What for?"

"For finding cats, dumbo."

"Who ever heard of a cat detective agency?"

"Nobody, so much the better. We're the first. The J and J Cat Detective Agency."

Jack began to look interested. "Why not Pet Detective Agency? Then we could hunt for dogs, too."

"No, the way to succeed is to specialize. You've heard Dad say that a hundred times. So we specialize, in cats."

"What if I don't want to?"

Jennifer shrugged. "Then I'll do it alone. The J Cat Detective Agency." She wasn't worried. She knew Jack wouldn't be able to resist being a detective, too.

She was right. As soon as their midafternoon dinner was over and they had stacked the dishes in the dishwasher, Jack said, "Well, let's get going."

She nodded. "I'll borrow Dad's map of Salem; it's in the car; and we'll figure out the territory." She felt in her pocket for the slip of paper Mrs. Eaton had given her. "She ought to be a cat that's easy to find. There aren't all that many silver blue Persians running around."

"Only she probably isn't running around," Jack said.

Jennifer grabbed a brownie out of the cookie jar. "Let's go. We won't find her hanging around the kitchen." She ran out the back door. But she had to go back in again, because Chloe followed her out. "You stay home. You don't want to get stolen, do you? You go sit on Dad's lap and watch the World Series."

"Cats don't like the World Series, silly," Jack said.

"Chloe does." She put the cat down firmly and closed the door. Through the screen she said, "Don't cry. We'll be back just as soon as we find Jasmine."

3

An hour later they had worked their way up to Essex Street, and they were tired. They had seen several cats, but no sign of Jasmine, nor of Joyous Melody Harrison-Eager, whom they were also keeping an eye out for. They had seen a black cat, a gray cat, one Siamese with a torn ear, a yellow cat, and two cats who were mixed, but no Persians and no Burmese.

Jennifer was disappointed. Three times she had even screwed up her courage to ring someone's doorbell, to ask if anyone had seen a Persian cat. One lady had been nice, one man had slammed the door in her face, and at one place no one had answered the bell.

"We've got to figure out a better way," she said. "We can't just wander around the streets forever. It's not scientific."

They walked on to Town House Square, and Jennifer bought a newspaper, to look at Mrs. Eaton's ad. "It's not here," she said, a few minutes later.

"Of course not. That's yesterday's *News*. There isn't any Sunday paper. It'll be in tomorrow."

Jennifer threw the paper into a trash basket. "Why didn't you say so, before I spent my money?"

"You didn't ask me."

They walked aimlessly then up Essex Street until they came to the Witch House. Jack wanted to go in, to get some information for his paper on witchcraft, but it was closed. They stood on the sidewalk, staring at it.

"I wonder if they really flew on broomsticks," Jennifer said. "That would be neat, wouldn't it."

"No, of course they didn't. It's impossible." Jack squinted at the big central chimney. "You know how they tested whether a woman was witch or not? Or a man, too, for that matter."

"How?"

"If they could say the Lord's Prayer backwards, they were a witch."

"Honest?" Jennifer thought about it. "You mean like you begin with Amen, and then go 'ever and forever...' Like that?"

"Hey, you can do it. You're a witch!"

Jennifer frowned. "Don't be dumb. Anyway I can't do it. I forget how it would go next." She felt a little uneasy. "What else did witches do?"

"If they looked at you, you had a fit."

She stared into her brother's eyes. "I'm looking at you."

Suddenly he shrieked and danced around. "I'm having a fit!"

Startled, she grabbed his collar. "Stop that!"

He doubled up with laughter. "Scared you, didn't I."

"No, you did not. I just don't like to see my twin making an idiot of himself in public."

They walked back to the square and then turned until they found themselves passing the house where the old woman had yelled at them. She was outside again, kneeling on a cushion, weeding the vegetables that were left.

Jennifer was wondering why anyone would bother to weed a garden in late October, when suddenly a long-haired cat ran past her, soared over the fence and ran for the house. The cat moved so fast, she was out of sight before Jennifer could react. "Jasmine!" she said.

"What?" Jack was down on one knee, retying his shoelace.

"A long-haired silver cat. She went into that house." She opened the gate, and then remembered how cross the old woman had been to them yesterday. As she hesitated, the woman looked up and smiled.

"Good day to you," the woman said.

Surprised at the new change in her, Jennifer said, "Hi," and then remembered that her mother told her not to say 'hi' to grownups. "Hello," she said.

The woman got up stiffly and came toward them, carrying a pumpkin. "How are you today?"

"Fine. Thank you." Jennifer glanced nervously at Jack, who was hanging back, ready to run.

"Would you children like a pumpkin for Halloween?" She held out the big, round pumpkin.

"Yes. Thank you very much." It was a beautiful

pumpkin. Jennifer was already imagining it with a mouth, a nose, and eyes. She'd put a candle inside and take it out on Halloween. Then she remembered the cat. "Excuse me, do you have a silver-colored, long-haired cat?"

The woman's expression changed. She looked almost frightened. "Cat? Oh, no. I don't have any cats."

"I just saw one run into your yard. I think it went in the house. We were just hunting for a missing cat, a Persian named Jasmine. It belongs to Mrs. Eaton, and it's been . . . I mean, it ran away or something."

The woman was backing away, not smiling any more. "No, it's not here. There are no cats here."

"But I saw one just a minute ago . . ."

"It must have been a stray cat, going through the yard." The woman turned and walked quickly to the house.

The twins looked at each other.

"That is one strange lady," Jack said.

At that moment there was an odd, agonized moaning sound coming from the house. The twins grabbed each other's hand. Before they could move, the door opened, and a large, silvery, long-haired cat came flying out, as if someone had used a broom to sweep her out of the house. The door slammed shut, and the cat ran across the yard, climbed the fence in one scratching scramble, and dashed past them.

By the time the twins had recovered from their surprise, the cat was gone.

4

"Anyway," Jennifer said, after they had searched in vain for the silver cat, "she was a lot bigger than Mrs. Eaton said Jasmine was. And she wasn't wearing a collar or tags or anything. And she could have been a he."

Jack was sitting on a stone wall studying the list Mrs. Eaton had given them. "And she ought to be bluer. Blue-silver. Anyway, you're right, I think that was a tomcat."

"But why did that old lady act so funny when we asked about cats?"

"Some people are allergic to cats. I mean not

just don't like them, but break out in a rash and get the jitters."

"But why did that cat go into her house?"

"Oh, that doesn't mean anything. If a window was open, he might go in. Chloe used to go to the Hallorans' house, remember?"

"Because Mrs. Halloran fed her."

"So maybe this cat smelled food or something."

Just the same, Jennifer thought, she would like to come back and take another look at that house. The old lady was probably telling the truth, but still there could be something about that house that attracted cats, and if there were, maybe Jasmine or Joyous Melody Harrison-Eager might show up there sooner or later.

They went home, and Jennifer began carving the pumpkin that Mrs. Bewitched had given them. It was a big pumpkin, round and firm. She was busy working on the left eye when her mother came into the kitchen.

"Where did you get the beautiful pumpkin, honey?"

"From the bewitched lady," Jennifer said absently.

"Who?" Her mother sat down opposite her.

"Oh." Jennifer looked up and saw by her mother's face that she had given the wrong answer. "A nice lady . . . well, nice sometimes . . . in the next block. She has a garden."

"You didn't ask for it, did you?"

"No, Mom, of course not. She just said would we like a pumpkin, and we said yes. Yes, *thank* you, we said."

"Why did you say bewitched?"

"Oh, I was just joking. Jack's doing a paper about witches."

"I know. And I'm sure he's found out that the whole witchcraft madness that nearly wrecked this town and killed twenty decent, harmless people, was started by some little girls, who apparently thought it was a joke until it got out of hand."

Jennifer nodded. She got the message. Don't go around calling people witches. Well, of course she wouldn't. She didn't even really believe in them.

When her mother had gone, Jennifer sat and thought about witches for a while, and then she got a pad of paper and began to plan the sign for the detective agency. Carefully, using a yardstick for a ruler, she made up the sign.

24

J AND J DETECTIVE AGENCY
CATS OUR SPECIALTY.
CALL US IF YOUR CAT IS LOST,
STRAYED, OR STOLEN.
WE'LL FIND HIM OR HER
IF IT'S THE LAST THING WE DO.

She studied it critically, her head on one side. Was that how you spelled "specialty"? She went into the study and looked it up in the dictionary. It was right. Go to the head of the class, Jennifer, she told herself. She decided to add their phone number, so the owners of lost cats would know how to find them. Then she crossed out "If it's the last thing we do," and put in the sentence she had thought of before: "OR DIE TRYING." That sounded as if they were really serious.

She took the paper upstairs to her room and got out a package of construction paper. Pulling out various colors, she made additional signs, one on blue, one on red, one on yellow, one on brown. Tomorrow on the way to school she'd pin them to trees and telephone poles where people would easily see them. And maybe after school she and Jack would put a small ad in the *News,* if they had enough money between them, and maybe they could get a free plug on that radio station that advertised lost pets. If they found Jasmine and got the reward money, they could start offering rewards for information about other pets. Just small sums, of course; maybe a dollar for a lead that really got them somewhere, or fifty cents for a promising clue. That was what her father would call reinvesting their capital.

5

The next morning she and Jack put up the signs. But that afternoon they put off the ad in the *News* when they found out how much even a small one would cost. They found Mrs. Eaton's ad, though, and agreed they could have said it better.

Jack suggested checking on some of the empty houses around their part of town, so when they left the *News* office, they made the rounds of all the houses they could remember that were standing empty. They tramped across overgrown yards, climbed up onto rickety porches, peered into dirty windows. Two were not locked, and when they went in, Jennifer wished that they hadn't. The places were dusty and strewn with cobwebs, litter on the floor, signs of tramps who had spent the night. She took several deep breaths of fresh salty air when they came out of those places.

When the house was locked, she would climb onto Jack's shoulders and peer in the window. Several times they found a skinny stray cat wandering around, but each was far from being pedigreed Persian or Burmese. Jennifer felt sorry for them, and made a note of the houses so she could come back and leave some food.

Finally, on their way home, as it was getting dark, they came once again to the Bewitched Lady's house. There was no light in the house, and it looked almost as spooky and sad as the deserted houses they had seen.

On the spur of the moment Jennifer said, "Let's look in the windows and see if we see any cats."

"You're crazy. That woman lives there."

"Well, you can see she's not home."

"Whether she's home or not, that's trespassing. It's against the law."

Jennifer was feeling cross because she was tired and because they had not found the cats they were looking for. "I'm not going to break in. I'm just going to look. That won't hurt anything."

"It's against the law. You could go to jail."

"Then don't come. I'll go by myself." She opened the gate, which hung crookedly on its hinges, and ran across the grass to the side of the house. There she crouched down for a minute, studying the place to make sure there was no light. Now that she was so close to it, she wished she hadn't come, but she was not going to let Jack call her a scaredy-cat.

She approached the house slowly. The nearer she got, the bigger and more scary it looked. No wonder that poor old lady was kind of odd. Anybody would be, living in a dungeon like this.

She stood on tiptoe outside a casement window that bulged out in a bay. She couldn't quite see in. Was there something around to stand on? After a minute she saw a wooden crate with a couple of squashes in it. She took out the squashes, carried the crate to the window and stood on it. It rocked, and she thought she was going to fall. Then when she grabbed the window sill, she felt a splinter jab into the palm of her hand.

Nevertheless, she steadied herself and put her

face close to the glass, to peer into the dark room. It was darker than she had expected, and she was not sure she would be able to see a cat even if there was one. She pressed her face right up against the cold pane.

Suddenly, she was looking directly into a face on the other side of the glass! It was a face blurred by the darkness, with only the wide glaring eyes staring at her, but so close that her own eyes crossed. She gave a small scream and fell off the crate.

6

Jack pulled her to her feet. "What's the matter?" he said. "What is it?"

Her teeth were chattering. "Somebody ... There's a pair of eyes..." She grabbed his hand. "Come *on!*" She began to run.

When they reached the sidewalk, he pulled his hand loose from hers and looked back at the house. "You made it up. The house is dark as pitch."

"I did not make it up. Go look for yourself. There were these awful eyes staring right into mine."

He stared at the house. "I wonder if houses really can be haunted."

"Oh, no!" she wailed. "I hadn't thought of that! That's what it was. A ghost. Just a pair of eyes and a blur where the face ought to be."

"If I could see a real ghost," he said, still half talking to himself, "wow, what a paper I could write for English! I'd get an A for sure."

She pulled at his arm. "Let's get out of here. You'll get an A anyway. You always do."

But he lingered, still looking at the dark house. "It can't be a real person, because there aren't any lights." Then he added, "unless somebody likes to sit in the dark. I guess it's possible." He made up his mind. "I'm going to take a look."

Before she could stop him, he ran back across the grass, set the crate upright again, and climbed onto it. Jennifer held her breath. She ought to go and take care of him. The ghost might hurt him. But she didn't have the courage. She stood still, and it took all her nerve not to run as fast as she could, away from that frightening house and whoever was in it.

A minute later he came trotting bàck, and she let out her breath in relief. "Did you see it?"

"Nah," he said. "There's nothing there. No ghost, no cats, nothing."

She couldn't believe what he was saying. "You *must* have seen it. It was pressed right up to the window on the inside."

"What was?"

"This blurry face."

"You said there wasn't any face, only eyes."

"I said I couldn't *see* what it was, but it has to have been a face. Eyes don't hang there by themselves."

He laughed. "You know what Mom would say? Your imagination is running away with you again."

"It is not." Jennifer was close to tears. She was tired and discouraged, and she *had* seen those eyes and they had been scary. It was upsetting not to be believed.

"I'm starving. I'll race you home."

She let him run ahead of her. She didn't care whether he won or not. Anyway she could win if she wanted to; she could run faster than he could any day.

By the time she had washed up and gone downstairs for dinner, she felt better. Her mother had made her favorite dinner, red flannel hash.

"We have had," her father said at dinner, "some rather odd telephone calls."

"What kind?"

"Don't talk with your mouth full, Jennifer," her mother said.

"Calls inquiring about a certain Cat Detective Agency." He looked over the tops of his glasses at the twins. "Does that ring a bell?"

"Oh." Jennifer exchanged glances with Jack. "Well, see, we're trying to find Mrs. Eaton's cat for her."

"Something," her father said, "about posters tacked to trees. A woman who claims to be concerned with the safety of local trees has protested."

"Oh." Jennifer was disappointed. "I thought maybe somebody had a clue."

"Someone else, aged I would guess about eight, also asked if you had seen a gray cat with black stripes and one inch missing from his tail."

"Was she offering a reward or anything?" Jack asked.

"Not that I know of." Their father helped himself to salad. "It would be nice if you asked permission before you broadcast our telephone number far and wide, don't you think?"

"It's in the phone book," Jack said. "It's no secret."

"But it's not in the phone book as a commercial enterprise. Where else have you put these posters?"

"Just on telephone poles," Jennifer said.

"I think that's against the law."

Jennifer sighed. Everything worth doing seemed to be against the law. "How are we going to let people know, then?"

Her father thought about it for a minute. "You might ask at the grocery on the corner if they'll let you put a poster in the window. If they won't, thank them politely and go away."

"What about that bulletin board at the super market?" Jack said. "Everybody sticks stuff on that."

"You have to get permission from the manager," his mother said, "and it should be a card, not a big poster."

"You aren't accepting money without results, I hope?" their father said. "I mean no down payment or anything like that?"

"No," Jennifer said. "But if we find a cat, we won't give it back till they pay us."

"Oh, dear," her mother said. "How would you feel if someone found Chloe and you didn't have any money and they wouldn't give her back to you?"

Jennifer looked down at Chloe, who was curled on top of her feet. "All right. If they can't pay, we'll give it back."

When she was clearing the table, she said to her mother, "Do you believe in ghosts?"

"I don't think so," her mother said.

"But you're not absolutely sure?"

"The older I get, the less I'm absolutely sure about anything. Is Halloween making you think of ghosts?"

"I guess so."

Later, she went into her room and closed the door. Chloe jumped up onto the bed beside her and began to knead her claws in Jennifer's shoulder.

"That hurts, if you want to know," Jennifer said. But she let Chloe do it, and in a minute the cat was curled up on Jennifer's chest, purring like a tea kettle on the boil.

Jennifer stared at the ceiling. She *knew* she had seen a ghost. She would go back and prove it. Maybe she could take a picture. Would a ghost show up on film? Maybe those awful eyes would, anyway. She wouldn't even tell Jack. She'd go back there alone. Even if it did scare her half to death.

7

Jennifer didn't have time to go back to the haunted house for several days. A week before Halloween was the twins' birthday, and their mother had arranged a wonderful party. It was half a surprise, since they had not lived in Salem very long, and Jennifer had taken it for granted that there wouldn't be enough kids they knew well to make up a party. But somehow her mother had managed to invite the boys with whom Jack had made friends, and some of the girls in their class whom Jennifer had mentioned liking.

One of the twins' presents, and the one that Jack especially was most pleased with, was the keys to the boathouse, and their dad's permission to take the boat out alone, as long as they didn't go out of the harbor. Jennifer immediately put her key on the gold chain she wore around her neck.

Jack would have liked to go out in the boat that very night, but it was getting dark by the time the last guests had gone.

"It'll still be there tomorrow," his father said.

So after school the next day they both went to the wharf. Jack tried to start the motor, and after a few spins, it did work. They put-putted out into the harbor, feeling grown up.

"You have to think about the channel," Jack said.

"This boat is too small to need to worry about the channel," Jennifer said. "Just so you don't hit a rock."

But Jack ignored her, as if she hadn't spoken, and went on explaining the rules of right of way as if she hadn't heard the very same things from their father. It was too nice a day to argue, though, so she let him talk on, and she leaned back, trailing one hand in the cold water.

They were having such a good time, the early autumn darkness nearly caught up with them. It was dusk when Jack remembered to turn back toward the dock.

"That was really nice," she said. "It's different being on our own, isn't it."

He nodded, narrowing his eyes to watch for rocks as he approached the landing. He slowed the engine way down, and Jennifer turned, crouching, ready to grab the piling of the dock as they came alongside.

They made a smooth docking, just as good as anything their dad might have done. Jennifer let Jack tie the mooring rope, willing to let him be in charge without any advice from her for once. It was her way of praising him for being skillful with the boat. She waited while he put the outboard motor in the shed, and locked up.

Another rowboat came around the end of the dock, heading upshore. It had no running lights, and she could just barely make out the figure at the oars. It looked like the old lady at the haunted house, but that didn't seem likely. Maybe all old ladies looked kind of alike. There was a gunny-sack in the stern of the boat, and as Jennifer looked at it, it seemed to her that it moved.

As the boat pulled away, she made out some of the letters on its side. It was the *Mercy W.*, the beat-up old boat she had noticed before. She tried again to see who was at the oars, but the person was facing away from the dock, and she couldn't tell who it was.

That night when the *Salem News* reported another missing cat, Jennifer and her mother agreed to put Chloe under what her father called "house arrest." The next day Jennifer got a big bag of cat litter, and Chloe's favorite food, and a new rubber mouse that squeaked, so Chloe wouldn't mind too much not being allowed out to roam.

"It's just till the thief comes to justice," Jennifer told Chloe. And she made a new resolution to find out who the awful person was.

That very day, on her way home from school, she saw a cat that she was sure was Jasmine. She yelled and started after her, Jack right behind her.

They chased the cat down side streets, through yards, around parked cars, behind trash cans, never seeming to gain on her. The more she chased her, the surer Jennifer was that it was Jasmine. She was the right color, the right size, the right kind of long hair. She kept calling 'Jasmine, here kitty kitty, Jasmine, wait.' The cat threw a few disdainful glances at her and kept on her way.

When they were quite a long way from home, Jasmine, if it was she, suddenly flew onto a tree and ran up the trunk and out on a branch, where she swayed dangerously.

"Now we've got her." Jack was out of breath. "I'll climb up, and if I don't catch her, you grab her when she comes down." But before he had reached the first limb, the cat had leaped over Jennifer's head and was off again.

She dashed into the yard of a large square white house with a wide front porch and up to the front door. Suddenly the door opened, and the cat disappeared inside. The door was closed at once.

Jennifer stood on the gravel path, breathing hard, staring at the house. Jack came pounding up behind her.

A cat, a different one, appeared in a window

and stared out at them. Then upstairs another cat's face appeared.

Jennifer looked at her brother. "I think," she said, "we've found the cat thief."

8

Jennifer didn't wait to think about it. She marched up the walk, onto the porch, and rang the bell. Jack edged close to the steps, ready to help if she needed him, and ready to run if that became necessary.

There was a delay, and Jennifer lifted her hand to ring again, but at that moment the door opened a crack, and she could see eyes peering at her.

"Oh, no! Not those crazy eyes again!" she thought. But these eyes were definitely attached to a face, and as the door opened a little wider, she saw that it was the face of a woman about thirty years old.

"Come in quickly," the woman said. "Both of you."

Jennifer took a deep breath and stepped inside. Jack popped in right behind her, and the door closed with a solid thunk.

"Mustn't let the cats out," the woman said. "What can I do for you? Girl Scout cookies? Money for the swimming team? What?" She was smiling, and to Jennifer's surprise, she looked quite nice. She was dressed in a very old pair of faded jeans and a white shirt worn open over a blue t-shirt that said "Cats...Cats...Cats."

As her eyes got accustomed to the dim light of the hall, Jennifer saw a cat, a Persian, sitting on top of the hall table. She thought it was the one they had been chasing. "Jasmine?" she said.

This cat had a dark mask, with black points and light silver ear tufts. She gazed at Jennifer with brilliant copper-colored eyes.

Another cat, bigger and very majestic, stalked into the hall. His coat was pure silver, with darker legs and face.

The woman was looking at Jennifer in a puzzled way. "Did you say Jasmine?"

Jennifer frowned at her. "You shouldn't steal

people's cats," she said severely. "It's not a nice thing to do at all. How would you feel if somebody stole your pet?"

The woman stared at her a minute and then said, "Maybe you had better come in and sit down. I think we've got a little confusion here."

Jennifer followed the woman into the old-fashioned living room. As she sat down, two kittens bounded into the room, and she saw that they had very faint markings like a tabby cat.

There was a coffee pot on one of the low tables, and a cup half full. "Would you like some tea or something?" the woman said.

"No, thank you." Jennifer was not going to let this woman, this cat thief, sweet-talk her out of what she had come for.

"I've come for Jasmine," she said.

"I *thought* you said Jasmine." The woman studied her. "How do you know Jasmine?"

"She belongs to a friend of mine. I'm going to take her back." She pointed toward the cat who had been sitting on the stairs and who was now a few feet away from her, still inspecting her with mild curiosity. "You've taken off her collar, but you can't fool me that way."

"You're talking about Mrs. Eaton's cat?"

"Yes." Jennifer was surprised and all the more indignant. Somehow it was worse to steal a cat from someone you knew.

"That cat," the woman said, pointing to the one sitting near Jennifer, "is Jasmine's brother."

"Oh, sure," Jennifer said. What did the woman take her for?

Jack, who had said nothing so far, went over to the cat, said, "Nice kitty," stroked her for a moment, and then picked her up and gave her a quick inspection. He turned to Jennifer as he put the cat down. "I think she's a he," he said. "It could be Jasmine's brother."

The cat pulled away, looking at him with hurt dignity. The kittens jumped on the cat and pulled at his ears.

"Well!" Jennifer could hardly believe such wickedness. "You've stolen the whole family. So where's Jasmine?"

"I wish I knew." The woman scooped up one of the kittens and held it in her lap. "I sold Jasmine to Mrs. Eaton. I raise Persians."

Jennifer gasped. "You're kidding!"

"No, it's true. I can show you my books, with

Jasmine's date of birth, her pedigree, the receipt from Mrs. Eaton. Or you could ask Mrs. Eaton. Or..." She paused and smiled. "...you could just decide to believe me."

Jennifer couldn't think of anything to say. She had been so sure, it was hard now to switch her train of thought.

Jack spoke up. "Those kittens look different from the others. It is because they're babies?"

The woman held the squirming kitten up for him to see. "The tabby bars are kitten. They'll fade out later. But these are actually different. Jasmine and her litter are Smoke Persians. The kittens are Chinchilla Persians." She went on explaining the differences in marking and in the various genes. She let Jack hold the kitten, who gnawed happily on his finger.

"We have a calico," Jack was telling her. "She was born in an alley."

"But she's not an alley cat," Jennifer said. "She can't help where she was born."

"Chloe," Jack said.

"Chloe Happy Singer James," Jennifer said.

Jack opened his mouth as if he was going to say he had never heard that before, but a look from Jennifer stopped him.

48

"That's a lovely name. Now why don't I make you some cocoa and show you the other cats, and you tell me how you happened to be sleuthing after Jasmine. Is Mrs. Eaton your aunt or anything?"

They followed her into the big, friendly kitchen and perched on two stools while she made the cocoa and found some chocolate cake with lemon frosting. Jennifer had forgotten all about her suspicions. She fed crumbs to Jasmine's brother, and told this woman, whose name was Esther Greene, all about the Cat Detective Agency.

They had such a good time, they almost lost track of time, but a chiming grandfather's clock in the hall reminded them, it was time to go home.

"Come back any time," Esther Greene said. "Come around at Halloween. The cats and I will have some goodies for you."

"She's nice," Jack said, as they left.

"Yes. Did you notice she has copper-colored eyes, too, like the cats?"

"I suppose you're going to tell me she's a witch too."

"Oh, no. Although if she was, she'd be a good one, like the Good Witch of the South. Let's remember to come back on Halloween."

They ran the last few blocks home, enjoying the cool wind blowing in off the harbor.

"It might snow," Jack said.

But Jennifer didn't think so. You never could tell, though. In a place like Salem, anything could happen.

She burst into the kitchen where her mother was cooking lamb chops and said, "Where's Chloe?"

Chloe answered the question by leaping into her arms.

"You are the most beautiful cat in the whole world," Jennifer told her, "and if you wanted to go to a cat show, you'd win every blue ribbon in sight."

9

The next day Jennifer and Jack went to the super market with their mother. While she was buying things for the last picnic of the year, which they were going on next day, Jennifer and Jack went to the manager with a neatly printed card advertising their agency.

He listened with a smile while Jennifer told him about the cat detective agency. "Sure," he said, "I guess you can put it up on the bulletin board if you want to."

"Thank you very much," Jennifer said. "There's one other thing we'd like to ask you."

"What's that?" His phone was ringing, and he reached out to take it off the hook.

"Has anyone been buying a suspicious amount of cat food lately?"

To the phone he said, "One minute please." And to Jennifer, "Suspicious amount of cat food?"

"Well, if a person stole a bunch of cats, he or she would need a lot of cat food. Has there been a sudden increase in the sale of cat food?"

"Oh, I see your point." He nodded. "*Very* scientific. I haven't noticed any increase, but I'll check around. If there is, I'll call you."

As they walked away, they heard him saying on the phone, "... couple of kids trying to solve the mystery of the missing cats." He laughed.

Jennifer looked back at him sharply. "I think we should keep an eye on him," she said to Jack.

"Why?" Jack brought out some thumbtacks from his pocket and began to attach the card to the bulletin board.

"I don't like his attitude."

"That doesn't make him a cat thief," Jack said.

"He thinks we're a couple of dumb kids."

"You know how grown-ups are. They never get the point."

"I'm going to speak to one of the checkout clerks about cat food." She dashed off and got in line.

Jack got interested in a science fiction comic magazine, and when he saw Jennifer again, she was helping her mother push the grocery cart to the car. "What did the checkout woman say?"

Jennifer made a face. "She said, 'Move along, little girl. I'm busy.'"

When his mother drove past the old woman's house, Jack said, "I'd like to get in there and interview that old lady. My teacher thinks that may have been Mercy Warren's house."

"Who was Mercy Warren, dear?" his mother asked.

"She was one of the girls who said she'd been bewitched."

"Mercy Warren?" The name seemed familiar to Jennifer, but she couldn't think why.

Their mother began to talk about the picnic.

"Are we going in the boat? It's the quickest way." Jack said.

"Boat!" Jennifer said. *Mercy W*. Was it the old woman she had seen in the boat?

"Are we, Mom?" Jack said.

Their mother gave a little shiver, and then pulled her coat collar up as if it were really cold. "No," she said, "it would be too cold on the water."

The twins grinned at each other. Their mother hated the water; it scared her.

To tease her a little, Jack said, "When we go by car, we cover about four times as much ground, the way the shore curves and winds around."

"But it's such a pretty drive, especially now with the trees turned."

Jennifer poked Jack and shook her head, meaning "lay off Mom." It was mean to tease her about being scared. Besides, if they went in the boat, Chloe couldn't go. But she intended to go down to the wharf as soon as possible to check the *Mercy W.*

As it turned out, Chloe didn't go on the picnic. Somehow she had gotten out of the house an hour or so before they left for the beach. Jennifer was worried. She went all over the neighborhood calling and calling, but Chloe didn't come. Jennifer knew from experience that she might be sitting calmly nearby, watching and listening as Jennifer hunted for her. She would come when she felt like it, not before.

At last Jennifer gave up and went back to the house.

"Don't worry," her father said. "Chloe often wanders off. She knows the territory around here by now. Cats are smart."

"I know cats are smart, but there's that cat thief."

"Honey, nobody's going to steal Chloe."

She looked at him indignantly. "Why not?"

"Well, be reasonable. The cats that have been stolen are pedigreed animals, right?"

Jennifer felt close to tears. "Well, if that cat thief's got any sense, she or he would grab Chloe in a minute."

Her mother put her arm around her. "I'll put some of her favorite food on the back steps. When we get back, I'm sure she'll be sitting there waiting for you."

Jennifer tried to believe it, but as her father drove across the Beverly bridge and along the north shore to their favorite beach, she kept looking out the window half expecting to see Chloe loping along beside them.

Somewhere between Manchester and Magnolia, Jack pointed to a weatherbeaten gray-shingled house that stood on a rocky point overlooking the sea. "There's the old deserted house," he said.

"What makes you think it's deserted?" his father said.

"I don't see anybody up there. And the windows are boarded up."

His dad gave it a quick look. "It'd make a pretty valuable piece of property. A little fixing up..."

Their mother smiled. "Don't get ideas, honey. Anyway it doesn't have a For Sale sign out."

He sighed. "I suppose. I'd sure like to have a summer cottage though." He had been saying this for years, first in New Hampshire, now here.

"Look!" Jennifer said.

"What?"

"There are three cats sitting on the porch railing."

"So?" Her father smiled at her.

"They might be stolen cats."

"Jennifer," her mother said, "not every cat you see is stolen. You're getting a fixation."

Her mother meant she was getting hung up on stolen cats. Maybe she was. She thought about Chloe again.

Later, in the sandy cove where their father was getting the fire going for the hamburgers, and their mother was putting out the rest of the picnic, Jennifer said to Jack, "Maybe tomorrow we could ride our bikes to that cottage and take a look."

"It's too far," Jack said. He was silent for a minute. "We could do it quick in the boat."

"Only we're not supposed to take the boat out of the harbor."

"I know." He kicked off his shoes. "I'll race you to the big rock."

She won, of course. Then they waded in the cold water until their feet were numb. By the time their mother called them to come and eat, they were starving.

After they had eaten everything in sight, Mrs. James took a nap in the warm sun, and the twins and their father went hunting for mussels.

By mid-afternoon the air had turned cold and it seemed time to go home. Jack and Jennifer craned their necks to see the old cottage, as they went past it, but the cats were gone and the place looked cold and lonely. Jennifer couldn't think why her dad would want it.

She could hardly wait to get home and see Chloe. She was sure now that her mother was right, and Chloe would be sitting on the back steps, curled up in a tight ball, waiting with a look of reproach, the look that said, "How could you leave me?"

As soon as the car stopped in their yard, she was out and running toward the back door.

Chloe was not there.

"She's hiding, to tease you," her mother said.

But Jennifer called and hunted for more than an hour, and there was no sign of Chloe anywhere. The food on the porch had not been touched.

10

Jennifer stayed out until dark, looking for Chloe. Jack joined her, and finally her mother and father came out, too. But there was no trace of Chloe, and none of the neighbors they spoke to had seen her that afternoon.

Jennifer couldn't eat any dinner. She wanted to hunt again in the evening, but her parents wouldn't let her go out after dark. They tried to tell her that cats do wander, and Chloe had not been outside for days.

"She's enjoying her freedom," her father said.

But Jennifer knew Chloe. That cat would never

let anything keep her from supper. Besides, she was spayed, and everybody knew spayed cats didn't stray.

Jack, who was almost as worried as she was, finally spoke the dreaded words. "Maybe she's been stolen."

Their mother tried to reassure them. "I'm sure no one would steal Chloe. Not that she isn't a beautiful cat," she said quickly, "but Chloe is too smart to let anyone make off with her."

That wasn't true. Chloe was curious. If somebody called her, she'd at least go up close enough to take a look.

"Call the Humane Society again, Mom," Jennifer said. "There's probably a night person on by now. They may not have heard about Chloe."

But there was no answer at the Humane Society.

"I'll call first thing in the morning," her mother told her. "I want you to go to bed now and get some sleep. It's been a long day."

Jennifer was sure she would not sleep a wink. But after about twenty minutes she was sound asleep.

She woke in the morning early, not sure for a

minute what it was that was bothering her. As soon as she remembered, she jumped out of bed, dressed, and went out to look for Chloe. Surely she'd be back by now. But she was not. Jennifer hunted until breakfast time, with no success.

When she came back, her mother called the Humane Society and the animal shelter, and then the radio station to put a notice on the lost and found announcements. She promised to put another notice on the bulletin board at the super market. "Try not to worry," she told Jennifer. "She'll come back."

"Jasmine hasn't come back," Jennifer said. "Joyous Melody Harrison-Eager hasn't come back."

"We don't know that," Jack said.

Jennifer put down the spoonful of shredded wheat that she had been about to eat. "I'm going to call Mrs. Thomas Fullerton and ask her."

"You don't even know her," Jack said.

"So what?" Jennifer glared at him, and he raised no more objections.

Her mother helped her find Mrs. Fullerton in the phone book, and even offered to call herself, but Jennifer was determined to do it. She had to take some kind of action or she couldn't stand it. The sight of Chloe's water dish and her empty food dish were almost more than she could bear.

"Mrs. Fullerton?"

Mrs. Fullerton sounded sleepy.

"I'm sorry to call you so early. I wanted to inquire if your cat had come back. Melody Joyous..." Jennifer stopped and corrected herself. "Joyous Melody Harrison-Eager."

Mrs. Fullerton's voice came to life. "Have you found her?"

"No. I'm sorry."

Now the voice sounded suspicious. "Then why are you calling me at this ungodly hour? If it's some kind of a joke, I can tell you it's not very funny. My daughter is heartbroken."

"Oh no, it's no joke. I'm a fellow sufferer."

"A what?"

"My cat's been stolen, too."

"Oh. Who is this?"

"My name is Jennifer James."

There was a pause. "You sound like a child. Are you a child?"

"You could say that." It always came up, the question of whether you were a child or grownup. As if that had anything to do with it.

"Well, I'm sorry about your cat." Mrs. Fullerton yawned into the phone. "Excuse me. You woke me up. I hope you find your cat."

"Thank you. And if I run across J.M.H.E., I'll let you know..." But she heard the click as Mrs. Fullerton hung up. She sat for a moment staring at the phone. Then she looked at her family, who were watching her. "She's probably a lot nicer when you get to know her."

"Come eat your breakfast, honey," her mother said gently.

It struck Jennifer that her family were treating her as if there had been a death in the house. But Chloe would *never* get hit by a car; she was too smart and too quick. Sometimes people put out poisoned food, crazy people who wanted to kill dogs, but Chloe wouldn't...She ended the thought right there, because she knew Chloe *would*.

Her father got up and began putting on his suit jacket. He had to drive down to the station to catch the train into Boston. "I expect by the time I get home, Chloe will be back." He kissed the top of Jennifer's head. "Try not to worry, Punkin."

When he had gone, Jennifer said, "Chloe is a

picky eater, even if she does eat a lot for her size. I mean she doesn't eat just anything."

"She'll try it though," Jack said. "She'll nibble at anything, to see what it is. Even Dad's pizza with anchovies on it. She took one bite and then washed her face for twenty minutes."

Jennifer burst into tears and ran out of the room.

11

Her mother let her stay home from school to hunt for Chloe. She couldn't remember any time, except when she was sick, that she'd been allowed to miss school. She was impressed.

Jack went off, cross because he couldn't stay out, too, but everybody knew Chloe was really Jennifer's cat.

Taking the map of Salem, Jennifer made a plan. She would go up every street and every alley within a radius of twelve blocks. If she didn't find Chloe there, she would start enlarging the area.

Remember to check out all trees and poles, she told herself. Chloe sometimes climbed too high and was scared to come down, although she hadn't done that for quite a while.

Her mother listened gravely to her plan. "I'll call everybody I know around here," she said, "and ask them to be on the lookout." She gave Jennifer three dollars. "You may get hungry. There's a McDonald's somewhere near Essex Street."

"I know where it is." She hugged her mother. "Thanks for being nice. Chloe and I really appreciate it."

"Be careful," her mother said as she left. "I don't want to have to come looking for you, too. Don't go into strangers' houses."

"I won't." As she started off, the sense of doing something made her feel better. Of course she'd find Chloe. And when she did, she'd get her a new collar and a leash, and when Chloe wanted out, Jennifer would go with her. She ignored the answering thought in her mind, that Chloe would hate a leash.

With all her senses alert, Jennifer walked slowly

along the streets, checking back yards, trees, alleys, any place a cat might have wandered. She covered the area she had planned with no success. Then she went to the house she thought of as The Ghost House and stood for a long time trying to get up her nerve to knock on the door. There were no signs of anyone or, more importantly, of any cat.

She was about to leave when she thought she saw a curtain move. A cat could make a curtain sway like that. Or someone looking out. Or a ghost. She took a deep breath and ran up the weed-strewn path to the big front door. Somehow it looked bigger and more forbidding than any door she had ever seen. She knocked loudly. Her heart pounded and she was having trouble breathing.

Nothing happened. She knocked again. This time she was sure the curtain moved. She leaned down and tried to look through the old fashioned keyhole.

The door was opened so suddenly, she nearly fell forward into the dark hall.

It took her a moment to get her balance and

to adjust her eyes to the dim light in the high-ceilinged hall. She looked up and found herself face to face with the woman who had given her the pumpkin. The woman was not smiling.

"What is it?" she said to Jennifer. "Why are you pounding on my door?"

Jennifer tried to speak, but her voice was doing funny things. She tried again. "I'm looking for my cat." She said it very fast, so the woman couldn't interrupt. "She's a calico cat; her name is Chloe. She ran away and got lost. I thought she might have come here."

The woman frowned. "Why on earth would she come here? I told you the other day, I'm allergic to cats. Now, if you don't mind, I'm very busy." She opened the door wider, inviting Jennifer to leave.

"I'm sorry I bothered you. I'm just so worried about my cat."

The woman's face softened. "I'm sorry, child." She seemed to be thinking about something. Then she said, as if she had just made up her mind, "I will try to help you."

Jennifer could tell she meant to be kind, but it

seemed unlikely that she could help if Chloe wasn't there. "Thank you anyway." Jennifer started to go, and then thought of something. "My brother is doing an English paper on witchcraft in Salem. He would like to know if this is really the house where Mercy Warren lived."

The woman hesitated. Then she said, "As a matter of fact, it is. My name is Warren. Agnes Warren."

Jennifer's eyes widened. "Are you descended from a witch?"

The woman laughed, a tinkly, pleasant little laugh that sounded as if she didn't use it often. "Mercy wasn't a witch. She was one of the children who accused the witches."

"But are you related?"

"Distantly. We...the house came down to us through my great-grandfather. *His* father was Mercy's second cousin once removed."

"Can my brother come talk to you?"

The long, bony face seemed to close up again. "I'm sorry. I am too busy." She was shutting the door, and Jennifer had to move or get caught against the door jamb.

"Well, thank you very much. If you happen to see a calico cat, I'd appreciate it if you'd call my house. My father is Stuart James..." She stopped. She had heard a sound. It was a sound she could not be mistaken about. Somewhere in that house a cat was meowing.

12

Jennifer stood on the steps looking at the outside of that very solid door. She couldn't hear anything now, but she was sure she had heard a cat. Why would that woman say there were no cats in her house, unless she had something to hide? Something like stolen cats?

But what could Jennifer do? She couldn't force the woman to let her in. Not even the police could do that, unless they had a search warrant. The police! Maybe they could help her.

She remembered seeing the police station not far away, and she set off in that direction, rehearsing over and over the speech that she would make.

When she walked in and saw the big, bald-headed sergeant sitting behind the desk, she almost lost her courage. But he looked up and nodded to her.

"'Mornin', young lady. Why aren't you in school?"

That threw her off. She hadn't rehearsed any answer to that. She hesitated, and then decided to tell him the truth. He listened, and then before he could answer, the phone rang and he talked to someone for a long time. Or it seemed a long time to Jennifer. She concentrated on counting to a hundred by fives and then by tens, while the policeman finished his conversation.

"Now then," he said, putting down the phone. "You want to report a lost cat, is that it?"

She was so relieved, she could have hugged him. "Yes, I'd like to do that. Also I'd like to tell you that I have a suspect."

"Is that right?"

She told him about the haunted house.

He smiled. "We've got a lot of haunted houses in this town, or so they say. Specially with Halloween coming up. We got a lot of elderly ladies who think they're descended from the early settlers too, witches and all. If that lady's got a cat in her house, I expect it's her own."

"But she said, she swore up and down, she had no cats. She said she was allergic."

"Allergic, eh?" He chuckled. "Well, they get notions sometimes, old ladies do. Harmless enough. I wouldn't pester her any more if I was you. I expect your cat will show up when she's got her fill of wandering. But if you want to give me your name and address, I'll file a report."

She gave him the information, but she was disappointed. She left, not knowing what to do next. She settled the question by going to McDonald's and having a Big Mac and fries and a milkshake.

Then she went home to see if Chloe had come back. There was no sign of her. A note on the kitchen table said her mother had gone to a luncheon for the Red Cross and would be home by three.

Jennifer got an apple and sat on the back steps. She felt tired and discouraged. Maybe a car had hit Chloe. People sometimes hit an animal and didn't even stop. Maybe she was lying in a ditch somewhere, hurt and not able to move. She got so upset thinking about that, that she decided to go in and watch television, to take her mind off it.

She watched a boring soap opera and had another apple. Then she got the pumpkin that Mrs. Bewitched had given her and found a candle and dripped wax into the pumpkin so that the candle would stay put. It didn't seem likely that anyone who would give them such a fine pumpkin would really be a cat thief. She must have been mistaken about hearing a cat meow. Maybe it was because she had Chloe on her mind that she imagined it.

Her mother still hadn't come home at four o'clock. Jack hadn't come home either, which probably meant he was in a pickup ball game at school. She felt bored and sorry for herself. Nobody was helping her find Chloe.

She got out the phone book and called Mrs. Eaton to see if by any chance Jasmine had come home.

"No, Jennifer, I haven't seen hide nor hair of her, and I miss her so. Your mother told me about your cat, honey, and I'm so sorry."

They talked for a while about cats and about

the weather and about Jennifer's school. Jennifer enjoyed the conversation; it made her feel comforted to talk to someone who understood how she felt.

After she hung up, she looked up Mrs. Fullerton's number, but then she lost her nerve. Mrs. Fullerton hadn't been too thrilled to talk to her that morning, and it didn't seem likely that the cat would have come home today. Still it didn't hurt to check. Jennifer decided to ride her bike up to Chestnut Street, to the address in the phone book. Maybe she would see Joyous Melody right there in Mrs. Fullerton's back yard, or peering out the window. Somehow she would feel a lot better about Chloe if she knew one of the lost cats had come home.

She got her bike out of the garage and set out for Chestnut Street. She had been on that street a couple of times, because her mother liked to look at the stately old houses built during the days when Salem was an important seaport.

It was a pretty street, with big shade trees and nice houses. A good place for such a beautiful cat to live.

After a few minutes she found Mrs. Fullerton's

house number. It was a brick house with white trim. There was a yard with a black iron fence closing it in. Jennifer stopped and straddled her bike, looking at the house.

As she sat there, a door somewhere out of her sight opened with a bang and a cat flew around the corner of the house. A girl's voice called, "Mel! Melody! Come here!"

A beautiful cat bounded up to the fence and stopped short, staring at Jennifer with golden eyes.

Jennifer was delighted. It must be Joyous Melody! She put down her bike and went up to the fence. "Joyous Melody Harrison-Eager?" she said. She held out her hand, and the cat came a little closer. "Here, kitty. Oh, you're so pretty."

A girl came running around the house. She looked about ten years old. She was calling the cat.

The cat looked over her shoulder at the girl, and then took a few steps closer to Jennifer. She sniffed at Jennifer's outstretched fingers.

"You stole her, and she got away and came home," the girl said. "Now you're trying to steal her again. Mama!" she cried.

For a moment Jennifer stared with her mouth open. Then she ran to her bike, grabbed it, and rode off as fast as she could go. All the way home she expected to hear police sirens behind her.

13

"I was thinking," Jack said the next day, as they were getting into their Halloween costumes, "that's just what those kids did to the women accused of being witches. They pointed their fingers at 'em and said they were witches, and everybody believed 'em."

"Without any evidence?"

"Of course there was no evidence. There's no such thing as witches. And that girl didn't have any evidence that you stole her cat."

"Because I didn't."

"But she believed you did, just because you

happened to be there. That's how it works, see? It's easy to get people into trouble." He adjusted his bat-man cape and swirled it a little. Then he looked at her. She had put on her mask and was transformed into a gap-toothed old hag. "Come on, witch, let's go. Have you got the big paper bag?"

Their mother came into the room. "Oh, you look fearsome. Remember, loves, don't eat anything till you get home." She didn't say so, but the twins knew she was worried about poisoned candy and razor blades and terrible things like that.

"What if Chloe comes while I'm gone?" Jennifer said.

"I'll watch for her."

"What if you don't hear her?"

"Honey, I'll hear her. Don't worry."

Finally they got started. They went up one side of the street and down the other, then over a block. People had all sorts of goodies to hand out, and it took quite a while to get their treats and to thank the people and sometimes chat with them for a minute. Halloween was almost as nice as Christmas.

At the haunted house they paused only long enough to look. The house was dark except for one light on the third floor. Jennifer had no wish to knock on that scary door again. They went on to the next house.

Toward the end, they worked their way down to the harbor, and sat on an overturned dory to rest for a minute. By the dim light of the street lamp at the head of the dock, they examined their loot.

"Pretty good haul," Jack said. "Tootsie Rolls, Almond Joy, Necco wafers, Mars bars, peanuts...I hate peanuts. You want to swap anything for three bags of peanuts?"

"I'll give you two peppermint patties."

"I'm giving you *three* bags of peanuts."

"So give me two. I don't care."

He gave her all three. "I wish we could eat some of this stuff. You know those people wouldn't poison us."

"We promised Mom."

"I know."

Jennifer looked past him, toward the street, and clutched his arm. "Look!" she whispered.

He turned to see what she was staring at. A

woman in a black cape was coming toward them. She was tall, and her face was hidden by a wide-brimmed felt hat pulled down over her forehead. She carried a large covered wicker basket on her arm.

"It's a witch!" Jennifer whispered.

Jack didn't answer, but she felt him tense up as the woman came closer.

Suddenly she saw them and stopped short. Then she veered away from the dock and walked down to the sandy shore. A rowboat came around the end of the dock, and the woman on shore gave a low whistle.

Jennifer and Jack sat very still, clutching each other's arms and watching. It was too dark to see clearly who was rowing the boat. It was a tall person in dark clothes, but it could have been either a man or a woman. Whoever it was eased the rowboat into shore, stern first, and held it steady with the oars while the woman first put the basket in, very carefully, and then climbed in herself. The boat went away along the shore.

The twins let out their breath.

"Who was that?" Jack was still whispering.

"You know."

"Who?"

"Mrs. Bewitched."

"From the haunted house?"

"Yes."

"What was in the basket?"

Jennifer shivered. "I don't know. I think it was alive."

"I thought so too. It seemed to move." He looked at her in horror. "Do you think it was a baby?"

Jennifer stood up and pulled off her mask. "I don't know. Let's get out of here."

They ran all the way home.

14

Their mother sorted out the candy and cookies, checking that the wrapping had not been disturbed. They waited impatiently.

"Did you have fun?" she said. She looked at them. "You seem quiet."

Their father came into the room and helped himself to a Tootsie Roll. "They probably ran into a few ghosts and witches," he said. "After all, this is Salem."

Jennifer didn't like to be teased about something so serious. "As a matter of fact, we did see a witch." She ignored Jack's warning kick under the table. "Maybe two of them."

Her mother frowned. "What do you mean?"

"Were they riding broomsticks?" her father asked. He was looking in the refrigerator, and after a moment he found a leftover piece of pumpkin pie.

"No, they were in a rowboat."

"Well, that's a switch." He grinned at them. "Leave it to our children to come up with a new angle."

"You think I'm joking but I'm not."

"Jennifer, I've told you before, I don't want you talking that way about people. Indulging your imagination at some poor woman's expense is not a nice thing to do," her mother said.

Now Jack was joining in. "It wasn't Jen's imagination," he said. "I saw them, too. They were really weird. They...one of them...had this basket and there was something alive in it..."

"I don't like this conversation," their mother said.

"We think it was..." Jack swallowed. "...maybe a baby."

Their mother put down a Mars bar. "Jack. I don't want to hear any more of this nonsense."

She looked at their father and shook her head. "It's not funny when they start leveling ridiculous charges at perfectly harmless people. Like that woman on Ames Street that they call 'Mrs. Bewitched'."

"That's who it was," Jack said. "It was Mrs. Bewitched."

"Jack! I said that's enough." She was really angry now, and the twins scooped up their candy and left the room. "And don't eat all that junk tonight," she called after them. "Four pieces each, that's all."

Upstairs they sat on the floor in Jennifer's room and carefully chose their four pieces each. "They don't believe us," Jennifer said.

"That's grown-ups for you," Jack said. "No imagination."

"It wasn't imagination," Jennifer said sharply. "It was real."

"Don't holler at *me*. I know it was real. I saw them, didn't I? I'm just saying grown-ups can't imagine anything they haven't seen themselves, that's all."

After she went to bed, she lay awake a long

time, worrying about Chloe. The more she thought about it, the more she thought she had heard a cat meowing, as the old woman walked by. What bothered her most was that she couldn't think what to do.

When the twins got home from school the next day, their mother had something to tell them. "I went to see the lady on Ames Street," she said.

Jennifer gasped. "Did you find Chloe?"

"Of course not, Jennifer. That poor woman doesn't even like cats. She's..."

Jennifer chorused the rest of her mother's sentence with her. "...allergic to cats."

"Why can't you simply accept that?"

"For one thing, because I heard a cat, when I was in her house."

Her mother looked at her, frowning. "I didn't know you were actually in the house."

"Yes, I was. And I heard a cat."

Her mother shook her head. "I'm sure you imagined it."

"How come you went over there?" Jack asked.

"I wanted to thank her for giving you that lovely

jack-o'-lantern, and I wanted to see for myself who this woman was. She's a charming person. She gave me two beautiful squashes from her garden. She is a very typical old New England lady, the real thing."

"Of course," Jennifer said. "She's real, all right. She's descended from Mercy Warren, the witch."

"Mercy wasn't a witch," Jack said. "She was one of the kids that pointed out the witches. I told you that."

"Well, that's worse."

"Yes, it's a very bad thing to accuse others without any evidence. That's what you've been doing to poor Miss Warren, and I want you to promise me that you won't bother her any more."

"Did she ask you in the house?" Jennifer said.

Her mother hesitated. "Well, no, she was working in the garden. But she was very friendly. I liked her."

"All right, but sometimes..."

"I don't want to hear any more. Do you understand?"

Jennifer knew when her mother meant business. She nodded. If she was right, Chloe wasn't there anymore anyway. And of course, to be fair, she wasn't sure it had been Chloe. She just was sure it had been *a* cat.

Jennifer continued to hunt for Chloe in the neighborhood, although she had little hope of finding her. Her parents, she realized, believed that something had happened to Chloe, that she had been run over or something else terrible. They began to speak, very gently, of getting a kitten. But Jennifer didn't want a kitten. She wanted Chloe.

Late in the week she and Jack went out in the boat after school. It was a gray November day, with a cold wind blowing in from the sea. Out in the harbor, where it widened to the ocean, the motor stopped.

Jack worked over it for a long time, while Jennifer sat huddled in the stern, wishing she hadn't come. Twice she suggested rowing ashore, but Jack was just like their dad, he was stubborn about that motor. But unlike their dad, he couldn't seem to get it going. In the end, muttering crossly, he got out the oars, and he and Jennifer rowed ashore.

The water was getting choppy by the time they reached the dock, and darkness was coming down early. Jennifer thought she could smell snow in the air.

She helped Jack lug the heavy motor to the boat shed and lock it in.

"Dad ought to get a new one," she said.

"Motors cost money." Jack was still feeling frustrated.

"I know that. I just said..."

"I heard you."

"Oh, don't be so crabby."

Jack hunched his shoulders inside his parka and stalked off up the street. Jennifer lingered at the dock. If he was going to be so grouchy, let him walk home alone. She wandered out to the end of the dock. The *Mercy W.* was there, pulling on the short length of chain that secured it to the piling. The chain was padlocked.

Looking down into the boat, she noticed a brown paper bag stowed away under the bow seat. It was a super market bag, a big one, and it was full of something. She looked at it for a minute, wondering what it was. If people were careful enough to padlock their boat, you'd think they would know better than to leave something in it that could be stolen. Unless of course they were coming back soon. She stared at the bag, trying to guess what was in it. What she needed was X-ray eyes.

Finally curiosity overcame her. She balanced herself on the edge of the dock, holding on with one hand to the piling and reaching down toward the bag. If she was careful, maybe she could see what was in it without actually moving the bag.

A voice behind her said, "Hey there."

She nearly fell headlong into the boat.

15

She caught herself just in time and turned around. It was the harbormaster. She had met him a couple of times when she was with her father.

"You all right?" he said. "Say, you're the James girl, aren't you?"

She had trouble finding her voice. "Yes, sir," she managed at last.

"Well, be careful or you'll fall into the harbor."

"I was just..." She had to say something. He was looking at her closely, and she knew he was wondering what she was up to. "Somebody left something in their boat. I was just going to see if...you know. If I should report it or something."

He glanced at the paper sack. "Oh, that's the Warren boat. Just taking something up the coast, I guess."

"Up the coast?"

"That's right." He put his hand on her shoulder. "You better get along home now, sister, or your folks'll be worrying. It's dark out."

"Okay. I was just going. Good night."

"So long. Say hi to your dad."

She knew he was watching her as she ran up the street. But the more she thought about it, the more she felt she had to know what was in that sack. It might be an important clue. And what had he meant about "up the coast?" Why should that old lady be rowing her boat up the coast?

That evening her parents put on their party clothes and left for a dinner-dance at Hamilton Hall. Usually she loved to watch her mother get dressed up, but tonight she was anxious for them to go.

The baby-sitter, a high school girl, was always so busy watching television that she didn't bother about them except to check on their being in bed with the lights out by nine-thirty. That meant that there were two-and-a-half hours between the time her parents left and lights out. Jennifer had made up her mind. She was going back to see what was in that bag in the *Mercy W*.

She would have liked to go alone, but Jack came out of his room just as she was sneaking down the back stairs.

"Where you going?"

She put her finger to her lips.

"Where you going?" he whispered. "I'm going, too."

Quickly she told him about the bag in the boat.

He looked disgusted. "So what? It's probably full of empty beer cans or something. Or tuna fish. Who cares?"

"I care. I'm going to see what it is. It may be a clue."

"Clue to what?"

"To Chloe."

He shook his head. "You are some kind of nut, Jennifer."

"All right, I'm a nut. But I'm going. Don't tell."

He watched her go down the stairs, but as she reached the bottom, he ran after her, silently, skipping the step that squeaked. He grabbed his parka from the coat rack in the back hall, and they went out into the cold, dark night.

"What if Jenny goes into the kitchen during the commercial to get a Coke or something and decides to check on us?"

"She never checks on us till bedtime. She thinks we're doing our homework."

They walked quickly. The narrow street looked different at night, more scary. Jennifer glanced quickly at the bushes along the sidewalk, as if she expected something to jump out at her.

"This is crazy," Jack said, more loudly than he meant to.

"You didn't have to come."

She walked along the curb, close to the few street lights. Inside the houses she could see people eating, watching TV, talking. They looked comfortable and safe. She was beginning to wish she had stayed in her own cozy house. The cold wind tasted salty in her mouth. In the distance a bellbuoy wailed like a deserted child.

"You want to go back?" she said.

Jack turned up his coat collar. "Nah," he said.

She broke into a run and beat him to the shore.

94

There was no one around, and the sky and sea seemed to be all one inky black mass. Not a star showed anywhere, and even the lights of the nearest houses blinked as if they were about to go out. The boats tied up at the dock creaked and bumped restlessly; further out in the harbor, sailboats and motor launches rode at anchor, eerie shapes only a little less black than the blackness that engulfed them.

"Watch out you don't walk right off the dock," Jack said.

"Why didn't we bring a flashlight," Jennifer said. She felt carefully for the supporting posts of the dock. Once when she put her foot out, she realized just in time that there was nothing but space and water below her. She gasped and grabbed the piling with both hands.

Behind her a sudden tiny light appeared. She whirled around.

Jack laughed, his voice sounding hollow. "Be prepared. I wasn't a Cub scout for nothing." He held up a tiny pencil flashlight that sent out a beam of light so thin, it hardly sliced the darkness. But it was better than nothing.

"Good for you," Jennifer said. "Let's work our

way down to the end of the dock. That's where the *Mercy W.* is."

As if to laugh at Jack's tiny light, a long narrow ray of light cut the distant dark in a fast arc.

"It's the lighthouse," Jack said.

"Oh." Jennifer was relieved. She had never been down here on a dark night before, and although she had seen the lighthouse beam from her house, it looked different down here.

"The fog's coming in," Jack said.

They found the *Mercy W.* where Jennifer had left her, bumping and pulling at the end of the dock. She felt around for the bow seat, holding onto Jack with her free hand. "Shine your light down here, can you?"

Jack tried to focus his tiny light on the area where the bag was stowed away. "You know what I think? I think the old woman's pushing drugs. It'd be a great cover: nice old lady, works in her garden, descended from the early settlers, all that stuff, but really what she's doing, she's taking cocaine or heroin or something in her boat."

"Where would she get it?"

"Where does anybody get it? Connections. She's

got a connection. The Witch House connection. Maybe she stashes it in the secret staircase at her house."

"How do you know she's got a secret staircase?" Jennifer's fingers touched the top of the paper bag. "Move the light over here."

"All these old houses have secret staircases."

She grabbed the light out of his hand and aimed it at the bag. She was leaning far out, over the bow of the boat, clutching Jack's hand to keep from falling in.

"The harbor master wouldn't be on to her because that's not his job. It's the narcs. What we do, Jen..." He was getting carried away with his idea. "...we find the evidence, see, and we report her to the narcs, and we get this big reward. Then I can buy a new motor for the boat, or even get that cat boat Dad wants, and we—" His grip tightened on her hand. "Somebody's coming." He pulled back so suddenly that she nearly fell flat on the dock. "Quick! We can hide in our boat."

They scrambled into their boat and lay down side by side. For a moment the only sound was the creaking of the boat as it rocked in the water and gently nudged the rubber tubing that ran along the side of the dock.

Then they heard soft footsteps that seemed to be just over their heads. They held their breath. The footsteps stopped.

16

It seemed like a hundred years before whoever was standing almost over their heads moved on to the end of the dock.

The twins breathed again, but they didn't move. In a few minutes they heard a scraping sound, and then the soft plopping of oars in water.

A moment later Jennifer sat up. The ghostly shape of the *Mercy W.* was fading into fog and darkness. "Quick!" she said. "We've got to follow that boat."

"Are you crazy?"

They were still keeping their voices low, because sound carried a long way across water, but Jennifer was busy with the mooring rope.

Jack pulled at her shoulder. "We can't go out in the dark. They'll kill us."

She knew he meant their parents. "This once, we have to. Get the oars up. Quick."

"If you think I'm going out in a pea soup fog at night, just to chase whoever it is, you're crazy."

"Then get out of the boat and go home, but hurry. I'll lose her."

"Lose who?" He had the oars up, and he made no move to get out of the boat as she cast off and sat beside him.

The oars grated and squeaked in the oarlocks as they adjusted their rowing to each other. The boat slid through the water, rocking a little in the swell.

"If Dad finds out about this, I'll say you hijacked me," Jack said.

"No, you won't." She craned her neck to look behind her. "Thank goodness. I can still see it. We need to row a little faster though. Not much, just a little."

"We haven't even got a riding light."

"You don't go out with all your lights on when you're trying to catch a crook."

He feathered his oar. "Hey, was there dope in that bag? I told you so! Wow! We'll get our pictures in the paper. 'Heroic Twins Capture Drug Ring.'" He paused. "But what if they've got guns?"

"It wasn't dope," she said.

"Then what was it?"

She turned again, caught sight of the faint riding light in the *Mercy W.* and adjusted their course slightly.

"Come on, Jen, what was it?"

She glanced at him. "Cat food."

"WHAT!" He let go of his oar and nearly lost it overboard.

"Cans and cans and cans of cat food, and a big bag of kibble."

His voice rose. "You mean we're risking our lives to chase some old woman that's got a load of *cat food?* We could be drowned. We could get lost. We could be grounded for months if Dad finds out we took the boat..."

She cut him off. "Hush. Voices carry, especially in fog. And row, will you?"

"Jennifer, you've got to be out of your mind."

"I'm going to rescue Chloe. *We* are going to rescue Chloe. And probably Jasmine, and make fifty dollars. And who knows how many rewards for other valuable cats. So row, and don't just sit there."

"I am rowing," he said.

"Harder. We're getting off course."

"We could be run down by a motor boat. At least you should have let me get the outboard..."

"And tell the whole world we're chasing Mrs. Bewitched? She's not stupid, you know. That outboard isn't exactly silent. Come on, Jack, she can't be going all that far, all by herself at night. We'll just see where she keeps the cats, and we'll figure out how to rescue them."

"And take them all home in a rowboat?"

"In a gunnysack if necessary, or a basket." She glanced at him and saw that he remembered the basket. "I'm going to get my cat... I'm going to get my cat..." She began singing it softly to the tune of "The Farmer's in the Dell".

Jack did some quiet muttering, but he put up no more argument. For one thing, they were too busy for that. The surface of the harbor got rougher and rougher as they approached the open ocean, and the fog began to swirl around them with confusing effect. Several times Jennifer thought she had lost the other boat, but then as the fog cleared for a moment she saw the light again. There seemed to be no other boats out.

She started to say that aloud and then didn't because she knew what Jack would say: nobody in his right mind would go out on a night like this unless he had to. But she had to. It was her chance to find Chloe. And Jasmine, and who knew what other sad and frightened cats.

She pictured them in cages somewhere, half starved, scared, homesick. But no, not starved, not with all that cat food on its way. If you stole cats to sell to somebody else, you'd probably at least feed them. But, this cat thief was not going to sell Chloe or any cat, because she, Jennifer James, was going to apprehend her and rescue the cats and get the thief sent to prison.

For a moment the picture of Mrs. Bewitched holding out the pumpkin and smiling flashed across her mind, and she felt bad about sending her to prison. But then she remembered how mean she could be, how she had said, "Git!" and pointed her bony finger at them as if she hated them. And all that lying about being allergic to cats.

"My arm's getting tired," Jack said.

"It can't be much farther." Her own arms were aching too, with the unaccustomed strain of pulling the heavy oars against the choppy water. The sea seemed to be fighting them, trying to drive them ashore.

If she let herself think about it, she could get scared. They were out of the harbor now, going along close to the shore line, but the waves battered them, and they had to keep heading into them to avoid being tipped over. Each time they drove into the waves, it took them off course. It was a slow, roundabout way to get anywhere.

Cold water splashed into the boat. Spray flew into their faces and made them gasp. She could feel Jack shivering. Her hands were so cold, she felt as if they were frozen to the oar and would never be able to let go. She flexed her fingers just to see if they still worked. They did, but they were painful.

They were rowing now in silence, their teeth clenched, giving all their strength and attention to keeping the boat from being swamped. Once Jennifer's oar hit a rock, and the old boat nearly tipped over. Without a word to each other they moved a little further away from the shore, to deeper water.

The icy water in the bottom of the boat made

their feet so wet and cold they felt after a while as if they had no feet at all. With one hand Jack grabbed the bailing can and tried to bail some of the water out, but as soon as he eased up on his oar, the bow swung dangerously broadside to the waves, and they shipped more water than he had bailed out. He threw the can down and went back to his rowing.

The black line of the shore was hard to see. Now and then a faint light in someone's house showed up, and at regular intervals the thin pencil of the lighthouse beam traced its quick arc through the darkness.

Jennifer was no longer thinking about the woman they were chasing, or even about Chloe. She was thinking only of keeping the boat afloat. She pictured her parents in deep sorrow because their twins had been lost at sea. Lost at Sea. Until now it had been a phrase she heard in a story. At this moment it seemed very real.

She turned to look for the other boat, and for a panicky moment she thought they had lost it entirely. Then she saw the pinpoint of light heading in to shore.

"She's going to land." She pulled hard on her

oar to turn their boat toward shore. "Let's go in real slow, so she won't see us."

Jack was staring at the shore line. "You know where I think we are?" He pointed to a cliff that reared up black as ink in the night. "I think we're about where that old summer cottage is. The one we looked at on the way to our picnic."

"We couldn't have come that far."

"It's only about a third as far when you come by water, maybe less. I think that's where we are."

They rested on their oars a moment, until the wind and the pull of the tide began to move them out to sea.

"Come on, let's get this thing ashore."

By the time they came alongside the dock where the *Mercy W.* was, they could see the woman's lantern as she climbed the steep path to the top of the cliff. Jack was right, Jennifer thought, this *was* the old empty cottage. Empty? Or full of stolen cats? She reached out to ease the boat up against the dock. Now what?

17

The woman had almost reached the top of the path by the time Jack and Jennifer had tied up their boat. Jennifer stopped to check whether the big bag of dry food was still there.

With the help of Jack's tiny light they found the beginning of the path. It was steep and rocky and overgrown with coarse beach grass. Clearly it was not used very much.

Behind them the dull pounding of waves against the shore made a steady roar. The wind chilled them, in spite of the heat of the climb.

Jennifer hated heights, and she had to force

herself not to look down. It seemed forever that they were scrambling up the path, clutching the sharp grass, grabbing the occasional wind-blown shrub.

When they finally reached the top, they crouched down and looked at the house. It was the old cottage, all right, its wide veranda facing the stormy sea.

The house seemed to be in darkness, but then Jack grabbed Jennifer's arm and pointed. There was a single point of light, moving slowly, inside what might have been the living room.

Without speaking they started toward it, keeping low to avoid being seen. They climbed the broken steps to the veranda and crept toward the windows. Very carefully Jennifer peeked in. At first she couldn't see anything except the small point of light, but as she went on looking, she made out a woman bending over. She was pretty sure it was Mrs. Bewitched. The woman was tall and thin, and she wore something dark, a coat or a cape like the one she had seen Mrs. Bewitched wear.

She tried to see what the woman was doing. Then all at once the old lady straightened up, and Jennifer saw cats. Lots of cats. They seemed to be eating. It was too dark to be sure what cats they were. As far as she could see, Chloe wasn't there, nor Jasmine, but there were a lot of dark, moving shapes.

The woman looked toward the windows, and Jennifer pulled back quickly. She put her finger to her lips and whispered in Jack's ear. "Mrs. Bewitched. Cats. Lots of 'em."

They stared at each other. What should they do? Jennifer considered the possibilities. They could storm in there and accuse her, and set the cats free. But she might have a gun or something. They could go away and call the police. But would the police come? They'd think Jennifer and Jack were just crazy kids imagining things. They could go home and tell their parents. But their mother liked Mrs. Bewitched. There was nothing to do but enter the house and confront the thief.

But while they whispered together, a different possibility arose. The door opened, and Mrs. Bewitched came out onto the veranda that faced the sea. Jack and Jennifer huddled together around the corner, trying to see what happened next, without being seen themselves.

The woman stood still for a moment, holding a Coleman lantern up at shoulder height, as if getting used to the darkness. There was no light inside the house now. After a moment she stepped down onto the path, and in a moment even the gleam of her lantern was out of their range of vision.

"Now is the time!" Jennifer said.

"What if she comes back?"

"She probably will. I think she's gone to get the bag of kibble. But it will take her a little while. It's our chance to rescue the cats." She went to the window and tugged at it. It was locked. She ran around to the back of the house and tried the door. It opened with a slight creak. "Quick!" she whispered. "Grab Chloe and Jasmine, if you see them, and let the others out." She pushed the door a little further. It was warped, and it stuck when it was just a few inches open.

She leaned her shoulder against it and shoved. It opened with a rasping sound, and she was inside. She heard Jack's breathing right behind her. Holding out her hands to keep from crashing into anything, she walked slowly across the floor of what seemed to be a kitchen. She made out the metal sink and the old-fashioned pump.

She barked her shin against a big iron stove and said "Ouch!" Her hand touched another door. She found the knob and turned it slowly.

She was standing in a large room. From the outline of the windows she was sure it was the room where the woman had just been. There was a soft scurrying sound all around her, and in spite of knowing it must be cats, her heart leaped into her throat. Something brushed against her leg and she almost screamed. She grabbed Jack's cold hand.

"It's only cats." She whispered it, and then said it again out loud. "It's the cats." She made herself lean down and reach around her until her hand touched fur. "There's nothing to be scared of."

"Who's scared?" Jack's voice squeaked.

"Turn on your light."

In this big black house Jack's small light seemed almost no light at all, but the shapes began to take on a familiar look. "At least a dozen," she said. "Look at them all!"

Some of them slunk away, close to the walls, one of them meowed like a kitten, several of them brushed against the twins.

"Chloe!" Jennifer said it more loudly than she meant to. "Chloe, where are you?"

There was a sudden rush, and a cat flew into her arms and wrapped its front paws around her neck.

"Chloe! It's you. Oh, Chloe! Jack, look!"

"Good," he said. "Let's get out of here." Then he gave a surprised "Oh!"

"What?" Jennifer was holding her warm, beloved cat close to her. "What's the matter?"

"It's Jasmine. Look. I'm sure it is."

"Grab her, and we'll let the others out, and we'll go. We can tell the Humane Society to come get the others..."

A sudden bright light shone in their faces.

For a moment they were too stunned to speak. Then Jennifer said loudly, "I don't care who you are or what you do to us, you can't have Chloe." She tried to run for the door, but the light followed her and blinded her. She ran into the wall. Behind her a cat squealed as Jack stepped on its tail.

She turned and faced the light full on. "You can't have my cat."

18

The person holding the light on them had not spoken a word. Jennifer kept one hand behind her on the wall. reaching everywhere to find the door. She had lost her sense of direction, and she could feel nothing but blank wall. Jack was standing close beside her, clutching a Persian who certainly did look like Jasmine.

"I've lost the door," she said to him in a low voice.

"I know," he said. "I could rush her and grab the light," he added in a low voice.

"She might have a gun or a knife."

The silence went on. It seemed to Jennifer that they had stood there forever. It was almost as if there were no live person behind the light, just that blazing beam that held them where they stood.

Finally she said loudly, "Whoever you are, and we know who you are, it is very wicked to steal people's cats. You must let them go. They are not your cats, and people are worrying about them." She put her other arm around Chloe, who was purring happily into her neck. "This is my cat, and my brother has Mrs. Eaton's cat, and we are going to take them home now, and let the others go free." She paused. There was no answer. "It is wrong to steal people's pets."

"I thought you were allergic to cats," Jack said. His voice was loud, too. They sounded, Jennifer thought, as if they were on a boat, shouting into the wind.

"Please turn off that light," Jennifer said.

Still no answer. The light stayed on.

Jennifer could hear her heart pounding. Somewhere on the house a shutter was banging in the wind. Cats rustled around the room. A thin black cat rubbed against her ankles.

Jack cleared his throat, as if he were going to say something, but no words came. In another minute, Jennifer thought, I am going to scream.

And then another light appeared, suddenly and without a sound. It was a soft light, held high, on the opposite side of the room. The bright light that was focussed on them seemed to waver.

A quiet voice said, "It's all right, Hattie. I'm here. You can put down the light. It's all right."

Very slowly the bright light was lowered until it was only a yellow puddle on the wooden floor boards. The other light moved toward the twins. Without that glare in their eyes, they began to get accustomed to the room. What Jennifer saw so confused her that she nearly dropped Chloe. There were two women.

In the dimness the two figures looked much alike, tall, thin, dressed in dark, old-fashioned clothes. The faces too, as Jennifer began to make them out, seemed alike. One of them was certainly Mrs. Bewitched, but which one?

"There's two of 'em," Jack said suddenly.

The woman with the lantern said, "That's right. We are twins."

"Twins!" Jack said. "*We're* twins."

"Yes, I know. We are identical twins."

"They can't have my cats." The other woman's voice rasped, like a voice not much used. She leaned down and picked up two of the cats, a gray cat with dark stripes and a big orange tomcat. They made no objection as she held them close. The tom nibbled a piece of her lank hair. At her feet several cats brushed against her legs.

"It's all right, Hattie." Her sister put her hand on the woman's thin shoulder. "Don't worry." But she herself sounded worried.

Jack spoke up suddenly. "Can she say the Lord's Prayer backwards?"

Mrs. Bewitched gave him a long, sad look. "She can barely say it forwards, young man. My sister is no witch. Surely you are intelligent enough to know there are no witches."

"Sure, I know," Jack said.

"Hattie, I left the dry food in the dining room, if you would like to give them some. You know how they love it."

The sister brightened a little. "All right. My old tom." She rubbed her cheek against the fur of the big cat. As she left the room, using her flashlight, she glanced back and said, "They aren't going to take me away."

"No, Hattie, I won't let them." When her sister had gone, she said, "When we were born, our mother died."

"How awful!" Jennifer had a sudden vivid picture of her own mother.

"My sister was injured...She has never been well. She was put in an institution for years. Now I care for her, and I have promised she will never be taken away again."

"But about the cats—" Jennifer said.

"Yes. She loves cats. They love her. She has only to hold out her hand, and they come to her. They are her family."

"But they belong to other families."

"I know, some of them do." The woman took a deep breath. In the wavering light of the lantern she looked old and tired. "Whenever I can, I return them. I took one back to Chestnut Street the other day..."

"Joyous Melody Harrison-Eager!" Jennifer said.

The woman looked blank.

"A Burmese cat?" Jennifer asked.

"I thought it was Siamese, but I don't know the breeds." She sneezed suddenly. "Excuse me."

"You *are* allergic," Jack said.

"Yes. That's one reason I bring Hattie's cats

out here. And she often stays out here with them."

Jennifer shifted Chloe to her other arm. Her right arm was going to sleep. "They aren't Hattie's cats, though." Her voice was gentler now. She was beginning to see how sad it all was.

"As I said, I return what I can. Some are just strays."

"You probably should take them to the Humane Society. That's where people go to look for lost cats."

"I have no car. Besides..." She looked away, and then back at the twins. "I have to trust you, you know so much already. If I told them about the cats, I'm afraid they would put Hattie back in the hospital. And I promised. She is quite harmless, you see, in every other way. And I love her. She is my twin."

Jennifer and Jack looked at each other. Jack cleared his throat, and Jennifer said, "We understand about that. Now let's see." She sat down on the floor, cuddling Chloe in her lap. Chloe turned on her back, her legs sticking up, and her eyes looking lovingly into Jennifer's face. "What should we do? How do we cope with this?"

Jack scrunched down beside her. "How about

if *we* went to the Humane Society, and told 'em how these cats seemed to hang out here, and that some nice lady's been feedin' 'em. Then the Society could come out here with its truck and take 'em in, and the people that are missing cats, could come and check up..."

"*Then!*" As she so often did, Jennifer was following his train of thought. "Then Mrs. Be—" She caught herself. "Miss Warren here could go to the Humane Society and adopt some cats for her sister. Don't tell them you're allergic, Miss Warren, and try not to sneeze. These would be cats nobody else wants, see? And they'd really need your sister. And she'd always have cats, because there's more homeless cats around than you can shake a stick at."

Miss Warren thought about it. "She might still go around town bringing home other people's cats. She doesn't understand."

"We'll keep in touch. Whenever somebody advertises a missing cat, we'll check with you, and if the cat is here, why, we'll get our mother to drive us out to collect it, and give your sister a stray cat in return. Our mother won't tell anybody. She's very reliable. Besides, she's already on your side. You talked to her and gave her some squash."

Miss Warren's face lit up. "Oh, that nice lady. Is she your mother?"

"Yes. So see, everything's fine. So now we'll just take my cat and Mrs. Eaton's cat and...oh, my gosh, we'd better get back home! Is it after nine-thirty?"

Miss Warren took a large gold watch out of a pocket and held it up to the light. "It's eight-twenty-five."

"We'd better hurry. We'll go out the back, so your sister won't get upset."

"You're very kind. You won't...you won't let her be hurt, will you?"

For a moment Jennifer thought she meant Chloe or maybe Jasmine, and then she realized that she meant her sister. "Of course we won't. Any lady that loves cats that much has to be a really nice lady. We promise, we'll take care of everything."

Jack marched up to Miss Warren and stuck out his hand. "We're pleased to've met you."

She smiled, and her whole face softened and

changed. She looked younger. "We twins," she said, "we twins have to stick together."

"Right," Jack said. "Have no fear."

They left quickly, as the sister's harsh voice called from the other room, "Agnes? Have they gone?"

19

They came silently in the back door at a quarter after nine. The trip back had been easier and faster, with the wind at their backs, but the cats had not been happy in the boat, especially Jasmine. Jennifer had had to hold both of them in her lap, while Jack rowed.

She put the cats in the bathroom, closed the door, and was under the covers, with her clothes still on, when the baby-sitter quietly opened the door.

"You asleep, Jen?" the girl said softly.

Jennifer closed her eyes tight and said nothing.

When she had heard her check at Jack's room and go back downstairs, she got up and let the cats into her room. Jack came in, too.

"We made it," he said.

Chloe jumped onto the bed and turned around in a tight circle until she found her favorite spot to curl up in. Her eyes blinked twice and closed. Jennifer stroked the velvety white patch on the cat's head, and Chloe purred loudly. Jasmine stalked up and down the room, managing to make it clear that this was not her house.

"I've got to call Mrs. Eaton about Jasmine." Jennifer went quietly out into the hall and listened to make sure the sitter wasn't on the downstairs phone talking to her boyfriend. The TV blared, but there was no other sound. Jennifer looked up the number and dialed it. She spoke softly, though she was pretty sure the sitter would never hear her over the TV. "Mrs. Eaton? This is Jennifer James. The J and J Cat Detective Agency, you remember?... Well, I'm sorry to call you so late, but I have good news. I've found Jasmine." She listened, smiling, to Mrs. Eaton's exclamations of delight. "Well, it's a long story. I'll bring her home after school tomorrow, all right? Or of course if you'd rather, you can pick her up anytime. My mom isn't here right now, but she'll be here in the morning." She listened for a moment and glanced at Jack who was trying not to look too eager. She made a circle of her thumb and forefinger. "Why, thank you, Mrs. Eaton. That's awful nice of you. Yes . . . Okay. Glad to be of service." She hung up. "We got it! Fifty bucks!"

"Wahoo!" Jack mouthed quietly. "Down payment on a new motor."

Jennifer put her face into Chloe's soft neck. "And a super deluxe new bed for you."

Chloe opened one eye, raised her purr to a louder pitch, and rolled over on her back to have her stomach rubbed.

"What do we tell Mom?" Jack said.

"She's not going to be happy about us taking money from Mrs. Eaton."

"I know."

"Maybe if we promise to dissolve the Cat Detective Agency?"

"Sure. That's easy. We don't need it any more anyway."

124

Jasmine leaped onto the bed and stared at Chloe with indignant golden eyes.

With her other hand Jennifer stroked Jasmine's ears. "It's all right. I just talked to your person. You're going home tomorrow."

Jack yawned and turned to go to bed. Jennifer yawned, too. The excitement was over and she was sleepy. "Go to bed. Me and the cats are ready to hit the sack."

When Jack had gone, she got into bed and curled up under the blankets. Outside, the wind moaned softly at the windows. But in Jennifer's room, all was well.